THE BISHOP'S CANDLESTICKS

The Bishop's Candlesticks

FROM *Les Misérables* BY VICTOR HUGO

FLEMING H. REVELL COMPANY
WESTWOOD • NEW JERSEY

Preface

Victor Hugo's famous story of the good Bishop of D——— and the thief who stole his silver suggests the timeless conflict between saint and sinner, between the worlds of ideal principle and existential reality—and the resolution of that conflict in transcendent love. It is a pleasure to add the story to our series of *Inspirational Classics*. We are grateful to Ruby Rhoades for adapting the narrative from *Les Misérables* with practically no changes from the original.

—*The Publishers*

Contents

So long as there shall exist, by reason of law and custom, a social condemnation, which, in the face of civilisation, artificially creates hells on earth, and complicates a destiny that is divine, with human fatality; so long as the three problems of the age — the degradation of man by poverty, the ruin of woman by starvation, and the dwarfing of childhood by physical and spiritual night — are not solved; so long as, in certain regions, social asphyxia shall be possible; in other words, and from a yet more extended point of view, so long as ignorance and misery remain on earth, books like this cannot be useless.

VICTOR HUGO

Hauteville House, 1862

An Upright Man

I · The Bishop Comes to D_____

WHEN MONSEIGNEUR BIENVENU CAME TO D_____
_____ he was accompanied by an old lady, Mademoiselle
Baptistine, who was his sister, ten years younger than
himself.

Their only domestic was a woman of about the same
age as Mademoiselle Baptistine, who was called Madame
Magloire, and who, after having been the servant of
M. le curé, now took the double title of femme de
chambre of Mademoiselle and housekeeper of Monseigneur.

Mademoiselle Baptistine was a tall, pale, thin, sweet
person. She had never been pretty; her whole life, which
had been but a succession of pious works, had produced
upon her a kind of transparent whiteness, and in grow-
ing old she had acquired what may be called the beauty
of goodness. What had been thinness in her youth had
become in maturity transparency, and this etherealness
permitted gleams of the angel within. She was more
a spirt than a virgin mortal. Her form was shadow-
like — a little earth containing a spark — large eyes,
always cast down; a pretext for a soul to remain on
earth.

Madame Magloire was a little, white, fat, jolly, bus-
tling old woman, always out of breath, caused first by

her activity, and then by the asthma.

Monseigneur Bienvenu, upon his arrival, was installed in his episcopal palace with the honours ordained by the imperial decrees, which class the bishop next in rank to the field-marshal. The mayor and the president made him the first visit, and he, on his part, paid like honour to the general and the prefect.

The installation being completed, the town was curious to see its bishop at work.

II · The Bishop's Palace

THE BISHOP'S PALACE AT D—————— WAS CON-
tiguous to the hospital; the palace was a spacious and
beautiful edifice, built of stone near the beginning of the
last century by Monseigneur Henri Pujet, a doctor of
theology of the Faculty of Paris, abbé of Simore, who
was bishop of D—————— in 1712. The palace was
in truth a lordly dwelling; there was an air of grandeur
about everything, the apartments of the bishop, the
saloons, the chambers, the court of honour, which was
very large, with arched walks after the antique Floren-
tine style; and a garden planted with magnificent trees.

The hospital was a low, narrow, one story building
with a small garden.

Three days after the bishop's advent he visited the
hospital; when the visit ended, he invited the director
to oblige him by coming to the palace.

"Monsieur," he said to the director of the hospital,
"how many patients have you?"

"Twenty-six, monseigneur."

"That is as I counted them," said the bishop.

"The beds," continued the director, "are very much
crowded."

"I noticed it."

"The wards are but small chambers, and are not easily
ventilated."

"It seems so to me."

"And then, when the sun does shine, the garden is very small for the convalescents."

"That was what I was thinking."

"Of epidemics we have had typhus fever this year; two years ago we had military fever, sometimes one hundred patients, and we did not know what to do."

"That occurred to me."

"What can we do, monseigneur?" said the director; "we must be resigned."

This conversation took place in the dining gallery on the ground floor.

The bishop was silent a few moments; then he turned suddenly towards the director.

"Monsieur," he said, "how many beds do you think this hall alone would contain?"

"The dining hall of monseigneur!" exclaimed the director, stupefied.

The bishop ran his eyes over the hall, seemingly taking measure and making calculations.

"It will hold twenty beds," said he to himself; then raising his voice, he said:

"Listen, Monsieur Director, to what I have to say. There is evidently a mistake here. There are twenty-six of you in five or six small rooms; there are only three of us, and space for sixty. There is a mistake, I tell you. You have my house and I have yours. Restore mine to me; you are at home."

Next day the twenty-six poor invalids were installed in the bishop's palace, and the bishop was in the hospital.

III · Works Answering Words

THE BISHOP REGULARLY MADE HIS ROUND OF VIS-
its, and in the diocese of D———— this was a wearisome
task. There was very little plain, a good deal of moun-
tain; and hardly any roads, as a matter of course; thirty-
two curacies, forty-one vicarages, and two hundred and
eighty-five subcuracies. To visit all these is a great labour,
but the bishop went through with it. He travelled on
foot in his own neighbourhood, in a cart when he was
in the plains, and in a *cacolet,* a basket strapped on the
back of a mule, when in the mountains. The two women
usually accompanied him, but when the journey was too
difficult for them he went alone.

One day he arrived at Senez, formerly the seat of a
bishopric, mounted on an ass. His purse was very empty
at the time, and would not permit a better conveyance.
The mayor of the city came to receive him at the gate
of the episcopal residence, and saw him dismount from
his ass with astonishment and mortification. Several of
the citizens stood near by, laughing. "Monsieur Mayor,"
said the bishop, "and Messieurs citizens, I see what
astonished you; you think that it shows a good deal
of pride for a poor priest to use the same conveyance
which was used by Jesus Christ. I have done it from
necessity, I assure you, and not from vanity."

In his visits he was indulgent and gentle, and preached less than he talked. He never used far-fetched reasons or examples. He would invent parables, going straight to his object with few phrases and many images, which was the very eloquence of Jesus Christ, convincing and persuasive.

He was the same in a cottage and on the mountains as in his own house. He could say the grandest things in the most common language; and as he spoke all dialects, his words entered the souls of all.

Moreover, his manners with the rich were the same as with the poor.

He condemned nothing hastily, or without taking account of circumstances. He would say, "Let us see the way in which the fault came to pass."

His conversation was affable and pleasant. He adapted himself to the capacity of the two old women who lived with him, but when he laughed, it was the laugh of a school-boy.

Madame Magliore usually called him *Your Greatness*. One day he rose from his arm-chair, and went to his library for a book. It was upon one of the upper shelves, and as the bishop was rather short, he could not reach it. "Madame Magloire," said he, "bring me a chair. My greatness does not extend to this shelf."

Monseigneur Bienvenu could be called at all hours to the bedside of the sick and the dying. He well knew that there was his highest duty and his greatest work. Widowed or orphan families had no need to send for him; he came of himself. He would sit silent for long

[13]

hours by the side of a man who had lost the wife whom he loved, or of a mother who had lost her child. As he knew the time for silence, he knew also the time for speech. Oh, admirable consoler! he did not seek to drown grief in oblivion, but to exalt and to dignify it by hope. He would say, "Be careful of the way in which you think of the dead. Think not of what might have been. Look steadfastly and you shall see the living glory of your well-beloved dead in the depth of heaven." He believed that faith is healthful. He sought to counsel and to calm the despairing man by pointing out to him the man of resignation, and to transform the grief which looks down into the grave by showing it the grief which looks up to the stars.

IV · How He Protected His House

THE HOUSE WHICH HE OCCUPIED CONSISTED, AS WE have said, of a ground floor and a second story; three rooms on the ground floor, three on the second story, and an attic above. Behind the house was a garden of about a quarter of an acre. The two women occupied the upper floor; the bishop lived below. The first room, which opened upon the street, was his dining-room, the second was his bedroom, and the third his oratory. You could not leave the oratory without passing through the bedroom and to leave the bedroom you must pass through the dining-room. At one end of the oratory there was an alcove closed in, with a bed for occasions of hospitality. The Bishop kept this bed for the country curés when business or the wants of their parish brought them to D———.

The pharmacy of the hospital, a little building adjoining the house and extending into the garden, had been transformed into a kitchen and cellar.

There was also a stable in the garden, which was formerly the hospital kitchen, where the bishop now kept a couple of cows, and invariably, every morning, he sent half the milk they gave to the sick at the hospital. "I pay my tithes," said he.

His room was quite large, and was difficult to warm

in bad weather. As wood is very dear at D———, he conceived the idea of having a room partitioned off from the cow-stable with a tight plank ceiling. In the coldest weather he passed his evenings there, and called it his *winter parlour*.

In this winter parlour, as in the dining-room, the only furniture was a square white wooden table, and four straw chairs. The dining-room, however, was furnished with an old sideboard stained red. A similar sideboard, suitably draped with white linen and imitation lace, served for the altar which decorated the oratory.

His rich penitents and the pious women of D——— had often contributed the money for a beautiful new altar for monseigneur's oratory; he had always taken the money and given it to the poor. "The most beautiful of altars," said he, "is the soul of an unhappy man who is comforted and thanks God."

We must confess that he still retained of what he had formerly, six silver dishes and a silver soup ladle, which Madame Magloire contemplated every day with new joy as they shone on the coarse, white, linen tablecloth. And as we are drawing the portrait of the Bishop of D——— just as he was, we must add that he had said, more than once, "It would be difficult for me to give up eating from silver."

With this silver ware should be counted two large, massive silver candlesticks which he inherited from a great-aunt. These candlesticks held two wax candles, and their place was upon the bishop's mantel. When he had any one to dinner, Madame Magloire lighted the two candles and placed the candlesticks upon the table.

There was in the bishop's chamber, at the end of his bed, a small cupboard in which Madame Magloire placed the six silver dishes and the great ladle every evening. But the key was never taken out of it.

Not a door in the house had a lock. The door of the dining-room which, we have mentioned, opened into the cathedral grounds, was formerly loaded with bars and bolts like the door of a prison. The bishop had had all this iron-work taken off, and the door, by night as well as by day, was closed only with a latch. The passer-by, whatever might be the hour, could open it with a simple push. At first the two women had been very much troubled at the door being never locked; but Monseigneur de D——— said to them: "Have bolts on your own doors, if you like." They shared his confidence at last, or at least acted as if they shared it. Madame Magloire alone had occasional attacks of fear. As to the bishop, the reason for this is explained, or at least pointed at in these three lines written by him on the margin of a Bible: "This is the shade of meaning; the door of a physician should never be closed; the door of a priest should always be open."

In another book, entitled *Philosophie de la Science Medicale*, he wrote this as a further note: "Am I not a physician as well as they? I also have my patients; first I have theirs, whom they call the sick; and then I have my own, whom I call the unfortunate."

Yet again he had written: "Ask not the name of him

who asks you for a bed. It is especially he whose name is a burden to him, who has need of an asylum."

It occurred to a worthy curé, I am not sure whether it was the curé of Couloubroux or the curé of Pomprierry, to ask him one day, probably at the instigation of Madame Magloire, if monseigneur were quite sure that there was not a degree of imprudence in leaving his door, day and night, at the mercy of whoever might wish to enter, and if he did not fear that some evil would befall a house so poorly defended. The bishop touched him gently on the shoulder, and said: *"Nisi Dominus custodierit domum, in vanum vigilant qui custodiunt eam."* *

And then he changed the subject.

He very often said: "There is bravery for the priest as well as a bravery for the colonel of dragoons." "Only," he added, "ours should be quiet."

To conclude: he was always and in everything just, true, equitable, intelligent, humble, and worthy, beneficent, and benevolent, which is another beneficence. He was a priest, a sage, and a man. We must say even that in those political opinions which often brought criticism, and which we may be disposed to judge almost severely, he was tolerant and yielding, perhaps more than we, who now speak.

In nine years, by dint of holy works and gentle manners, Monseigneur Bienvenu had filled the City of D——— with a kind of tender and filial veneration.

---

* Unless God protects a house, they who guard it, watch in vain.

Even his conduct towards Napoleon had been accepted and pardoned in silence by the people, a good, weak flock, who adored their emperor, but who loved their bishop.

V · What He Believed

WE NEED NOT EXAMINE THE BISHOP OF D———
from an orthodox point of view. Before such a soul, we
feel only in the humour of respect. The conscience of
an upright man should be taken for granted. Moreover,
given certain natures, and we admit the possible de-
velopment of all the beauties of human virtues in a
faith different from our own.

What he thought of this dogma or that mystery, are
secrets of the interior faith known only in the tomb
where souls enter stripped of all externals. But we are
sure that religious difficulties never resulted with him
in hypocrisy. No corruption is possible with the dia-
mond. He believed as much as he could. *Credo in
Patrem,* he often exclaimed; and, besides, he derived
from his good deeds that measure of satisfaction which
meets the demands of conscience, and which says in a
low voice, "thou art with God."

We think it our duty to notice that, outside of and,
so to say, beyond his faith, the bishop had an excess of
love. It is on that account, *quia multum amavit,* that he
was deemed vulnerable by "serious men," "sober persons," and "reasonable people"; favourite phrases in our
sad world, where egotism receives its key-note from
pedantry. What was this excess of love? It was a serene

benevolence, overflowing men, as we have already indicated, and, on occasion, extending to inanimate things. He lived without disdain. He was indulgent to God's creation. Every man, even the best, has some inconsiderate severity which he holds in reserve for animals. The Bishop of D——— had none of this severity peculiar to most priests. Ugliness of aspect, monstrosities of instinct, did not trouble or irritate him. He was moved and afflicted by it. He seemed to be thoughtfully seeking, beyond the apparent life, for its cause, its explanation, or its excuse. He seemed at times to ask changes of God. He examined without passion, and with the eye of a linguist deciphering a palimpsest, the portion of chaos which there is yet in nature. These reveries sometimes drew from him strange words. One morning, he was in his garden, and thought himself alone; but his sister was walking behind him; all at once he stopped and looked at something on the ground: it was a large, black, hairy, horrible spider. His sister heard him say:

"Poor thing! it is not his fault."

Why not relate this almost divine childlikeness of goodness? Puerilities, perhaps, but these sublime puerilities were those of St. Francis of Assisi and of Marcus Aurelius. One day he received a sprain rather than crush an ant.

So lived this upright man. Sometimes he went to sleep in his garden, and then there was nothing more venerable.

Monseigneur Bienvenu had been formerly, according to the accounts of his youth and even his early manhood, a passionate, perhaps a violent, man. His universal tenderness was less an instinct of nature than the result of a strong conviction filtered through life into his heart, slowly dropping in upon him, thought by thought; for a character, as well as a rock, may be worn into by drops of water. Such marks are ineffaceable; such formations are indestructible.

In 1815, we think we have already said, he attained his seventy-sixth year, but he did not appear to be more than sixty. He was not tall; he was somewhat fleshy, and frequently took long walks that he might not become more so; he had a firm step, and was but little bowed; a circumstance from which we do not claim to draw any conclusion.

When he talked with that infantile gaiety that was one of his graces, and of which we have already spoken, all felt at ease in his presence, and from his whole person joy seemed to radiate, his ruddy and fresh complexion, and his white teeth, all of which were well preserved, and which he showed when he laughed, gave him that open and easy air which makes us say of a man: he is a good fellow; and of an old man: he is a good man. At the first view, and to one who saw him for the first time, he was nothing more than a good man. But if one spent a few hours with him, and saw him in a thoughtful mood, little by little the good man became transfigured, and became ineffably imposing; his large and serious forehead, rendered noble by his white hair, became noble also by meditation; majesty was developed from this goodness, yet the radiance of goodness remained; and one felt something of the emotion that he would experience in seeing a smiling angel slowly spread his wings without ceasing to smile. Respect, unutterable respect, penetrated you by degrees, and made its way to your heart; and you felt that you had before you one of those strong, tried, and indulgent souls, where the thought is so great that it cannot be other than gentle.

He did not attempt to make his robe assume the folds of Elijah's mantle; he cast no ray of the future upon the dark scroll of events; he sought not to condense into a flame the glimmer of things; he had nothing of the prophet and nothing of the magician. His humble soul loved; that was all.

The Fall

I · *The Night of a Day's Tramp*

AN HOUR BEFORE SUNSET, ON THE EVENING OF A
day in the beginning of October, 1815, a man travel-
ling afoot entered the little town of D———. The
few persons who at this time were at their windows or
their doors, regarded this traveller with a sort of dis-
trust. It would have been hard to find a passer-by more
wretched in appearance. He was a man of middle height,
stout and hardy, in the strength of maturity; he might
have been forty-six or seven. A slouched leather cap
half hid his face, bronzed by the sun and wind, and
dripping with sweat. His shaggy breast was seen through
the coarse yellow shirt which at the neck was fastened
by a small silver anchor; he wore a cravat twisted like
a rope; coarse blue trousers, worn and shabby, white on
one knee, and with holes in the other; an old ragged
grey blouse, patched on one side with a piece of green
cloth sewed with twine: upon his back was a well-filled
knapsack, strongly buckled and quite new. In his hand
he carried an enormous knotted stick: his stockingless
feet were in hobnailed shoes; his hair was cropped and
his beard long.

The sweat, the heat, his long walk, and the dust,
added an indescribable meanness to his tattered appearance.

His hair was shorn, but bristly, for it had begun to grow a little, and seemingly had not been cut for some time. Nobody knew him; he was evidently a traveller. Whence had he come? From the south—perhaps from the sea; for he was making his entrance into D——— by the same road by which, seven months before, the Emperor Napoleon went from Cannes to Paris. This man must have walked all day long; for he appeared very weary. Some women of the old city which is at the lower part of the town, had seen him stop under the trees of the boulevard Gassendi, and drink at the fountain which is at the end of the promenade. He must have been very thirsty, for some children who followed him, saw him stop not two hundred steps further on and drink again at the fountain in the market-place.

When he reached the corner of the Rue Poichevert he turned to the left and went towards the mayor's office. He went in, and a quarter of an hour afterwards he came out.

It was about eight o'clock in the evening: as he did not know the streets, he walked at hazard.

So he came to the prefecture, then to the seminary; on passing by the Cathedral square, he shook his fist at the church.

At the corner of this square stands a printing-office; there were first printed the proclamations of the emperor, and the Imperial Guard to the army, brought from the island of Elba, and dictated by Napoleon himself.

Exhausted with fatigue, and hoping for nothing

better, he lay down on a stone bench in front of this printing-office.

Just then an old woman came out of the church. She saw the man lying there in the dark and said:

"What are you doing there, my friend?"

He replied harshly, and with anger in his tone:

"You see, my good woman, I am going to sleep."

The good woman, who really merited the name, was Madame la Marquise de R———.

"Upon the bench?" said she.

"For nineteen years I have had a wooden mattress," said the man; "to-night I have a stone one."

"You have been a soldier?"

"Yes, my good woman, a soldier."

"Why don't you go to the inn?"

"Because I have no money." Which, of course, was not the truth, but his money had not been found acceptable in any place of lodging in the City of D———.

"Alas!" said Madame de R———, "I have only four sous in my purse."

"Give them then." The man took the four sous, and Madame de R——— continued:

"You cannot find lodging for so little in an inn. But have you tried? You cannot pass the night so. You must be cold and hungry. They should give you lodging for charity."

"I have knocked at every door."

"Well, what then?"

"Everybody has driven me away."

The good woman touched the man's arm and pointed

[28]

out to him, on the other side of the square, a little low
house beside the bishop's palace.

"You have knocked at every door?"

"Yes."

"Have you knocked at that one there?"

"No."

"Knock there."

II · *Prudence Commended to Wisdom*

THAT EVENING, AFTER HIS WALK IN THE TOWN, the Bishop of D——— remained quite late in his room. He was busy with his great work on Duty, which unfortunately is left incomplete.

At eight o'clock he was still at work writing with some inconvenience on little slips of paper, with a large book open on his knees, when Madame Magloire, as usual, came in to take the silver from the panel near the bed. A moment after, the bishop, knowing that the table was laid, and that his sister was perhaps waiting, closed his book and went into the dining room.

This dining-room was an oblong apartment, with a fireplace, and with a door upon the street, as we have said, and a window opening into the garden.

Madame Magloire had just finished placing the plates.

While she was arranging the table, she was talking with Mademoiselle Baptistine.

The lamp was on the table, which was near the fireplace, where a good fire was burning.

Just as the bishop entered, Madame Magloire was speaking with some warmth. She was talking to *Mademoiselle* upon a familiar subject, and one to which the bishop was quite accustomed. It was discussion on the means of fastening the front door.

It seems that while Madame Magloire was out making provision for supper, she had heard the news in sundry places. There was talk that an ill-favoured runaway, a suspicious vagabond, had arrived and was lurking somewhere in the town, and that some unpleasant adventures might befall those who should come home late that night; besides that the police were very bad, as the prefect and the mayor did not like one another, and were hoping to injure each other by untoward events; that it was the part of wise people to be their own police, and to protect their own persons; and that every one ought to be careful to shut up, bolt, and bar his house properly, and *secure his door thoroughly.*

Then Madame Magloire told of the story passing about in the market-place. It appeared that a bare-footed gipsy man, a sort of dangerous beggar, was in the town. He had gone for lodging to Jacquin Labarre, who had refused to receive him; he had been seen to enter the town by the boulevard Gassendi, and to roam though the street at dusk. A man with a knapsack and a rope, and a terrible-looking face.

"Indeed!" said the bishop.

This readiness to question her encouraged Madame Magloire; it seemed to indicate that the bishop was really well-nigh alarmed. She continued triumphantly: "Yes, monseigneur; it is true. There will something happen to-night in the town: everybody says so. The police are so badly organised (a convenient repetition). To live in this mountainous country, and not even to have street

[31]

lamps! If one goes out, it is dark as a pocket. And I say, monseigneur, and mademoiselle says also—"

"Me?" interrupted the sister; "I say nothing. Whatever my brother does is well done."

Madame Magloire went on as if she had not heard this protestation:

"We might say this house is not safe at all; and if monseigneur will permit, I will go and tell Paulin Musebois, the locksmith, to come and put the old bolts in the door again; they are there, and it will take but a minute. I say we must have bolts, were it only for to-night; for I say that a door which opens by a latch on the outside to the first comer, nothing could be more horrible: and then monseigneur has the habit of always saying 'Come in,' even at midnight. But, my goodness! there is no need even to ask leave—"

At this moment there was a violent knock on the door.

"Come in!" said the bishop.

III · *The Heroism of Passive Obedience*

THE DOOR OPENED.

It opened quickly, quite wide, as if pushed by some one boldly and with energy.

A man entered.

That man, we know already; it was the traveller we have seen wandering about in search of a lodging.

He came in, took one step, and paused, leaving the door open behind him. He had his knapsack on his back, his stick in his hand, and a rough, hard, tired, and fierce look in his eyes, as seen by the firelight. He was hideous. It was an apparition of ill omen.

Madame Magloire had not even the strength to scream. She stood trembling with her mouth open.

Mademoiselle Baptistine turned, saw the man enter, and started up half alarmed; then, slowly turning back again towards the fire, she looked at her brother, and her face resumed its usual calmness and serenity.

The bishop looked upon the man with a tranquil eye.

As he was opening his mouth to speak, doubtless to ask the stranger what he wanted, the man, leaning with both hands on his club, glanced from one to another in turn, and without waiting for the bishop to speak, said in a loud voice:

"See here! My name is Jean Valjean. I am a convict;

I have been nineteen years in the galleys. Four days ago I was set free, and started for Pontarlier, which is my destination; during those four days I have walked from Toulon. To-day I have walked twelve leagues. When I reached this place this evening I went to an inn, and they sent me away on account of my yellow passport, which I had shown at the mayor's office, as was necessary. I went to another inn; they said: 'Get out!' It was the same with one as with another; nobody would have me. I went to the prison, and the turnkey would not let me in. I crept into a dog-kennel, the dog bit me, and drove me away as if he had been a man; you would have said that he knew who I was. I went into the fields to sleep beneath the stars: there were no stars; I thought it would rain, and there was no good God to stop the drops so I came back to the town to get the shelter of some doorway. There in the square I lay down upon a stone; a good woman showed me your house, and said; 'Knock there!' I have knocked. What is this place? Are you an inn? I have money; my savings, one hundred and nine francs and fifteen sous which I have earned in the galleys by my work for nineteen years. I will pay. What do I care? I have money. I am very tired—twelve leagues on foot, and I am so hungry. Can I stay?"

"Madame Magloire," said the bishop, "put on another plate."

The man took three steps, and came near the lamp which stood on the table. "Stop," he exclaimed; as if he had not been understood, "not that, did you understand me? I am a galley-slave—a convict—I am just from the galleys." He drew from his pocket a large sheet of yellow paper, which he unfolded. "There is my passport, yellow as you see. That is enough to have me kicked out wherever I go. Will you read it? I know how to read, I do. I learned in the galleys. There is a school there for those who care for it. See, here is what they have put in the passport: 'Jean Valjean, a liberated convict, native of ———,' you don't care for that, 'has been nineteen years in the galleys; five years for burglary; fourteen years for having attempted four times to escape. This man is very dangerous.' There you have it! Everybody has thrust me out; will you receive me? Is this an inn? Can you give me something to eat, and a place to sleep? Have you a stable?"

"Madame Magloire," said the bishop, "put some sheets on the bed in the alcove."

We have already described the kind of obedience yielded by these two women.

Madame Magloire went out to fulfil her orders.

The bishop turned to the man:

"Monsieur, sit down and warm yourself: we are going to take supper presently, and your bed will be made ready while you sup."

At last the man quite understood; his face, the expression of which till then had been gloomy and hard, now expressed stupefaction, doubt, and joy, and became absolutely wonderful. He began to stutter like a madman.

"True? What! You will keep me? you won't drive me away? a convict! You call me *Monsieur* and don't say 'Get out, dog!' as everybody else does. I thought that you would send me away, so I told first off who I am. Oh! the fine woman who sent me here! I shall have a supper! a bed like other people with mattress and sheets—a bed! It is nineteen years that I have not slept on a bed. You are really willing that I should stay? You are good people! Besides I have money: I will pay well. I beg your pardon, Monsieur Innkeeper, what is your name? I will pay all you say. You are a fine man. You are an innkeeper, an't you?"

"I am a priest who lives here," said the bishop.

"A priest," said the man. "Oh, noble priest! Then you do not ask any money? You are the curé, an't you? the curé of this big church? Yes, that's it. How stupid I am; I didn't notice your cap."

While speaking, he had deposited his knapsack and stick in the corner, replaced his passport in his pocket, and sat down. Mademoiselle Baptistine looked at him pleasantly. He continued:

"You are humane, Monsieur Curé; you don't despise me. A good priest is a good thing. Then you don't want me to pay you?"

"No," said the bishop, "keep your money. How much have you? You said a hundred and nine francs, I think."

"And fifteen sous," added the man.

"One hundred and nine francs and fifteen sous. And how long did it take you to earn that?"

"Nineteen years."

"Nineteen years!"

The bishop sighed deeply.

[36]

The man continued: "I have all my money yet. In four days I have spent only twenty-five sous which I earned by unloading wagons at Grasse. As you are an abbé, I must tell you, we have an almoner in the galleys. And then one day I saw a bishop; monseigneur, they called him. It was the Bishop of Majore from Marseilles. He is the curé who is over the curés. You see —beg pardon, how I bungle saying it, but for me, it is so far off! you know what we are. He said mass in the centre of the place on an altar; he had a pointed gold thing on his head, that shone in the sun; it was noon. We were drawn up in line on three sides, with cannons and matches lighted before us. We could not see him well. He spoke to us, but he was not near enough, we did not understand him. That is what a bishop is."

While he was talking, the bishop shut the door, which he had left wide open.

Madame Magloire brought in a plate and set it on the table.

"Madame Magloire," said the bishop, "put this plate as near the fire as you can." Then turning towards his guest, he added: "The night wind is raw in the Alps; you must be cold, monsieur."

Every time he said this word monsieur, with his gently solemn, and heartily hospitable voice, the man's countenance lighted up. *Monsieur* to a convict, is a glass of water to a man dying of thirst at sea. Ignominy thirsts for respect.

"The lamp," said the bishop, "gives a very poor light."

Madame Magloire understood him, and going to his bedchamber, took from the mantel the two silver candlesticks, lighted the candles, and placed them on the table.

"Monsieur Curé," said the man, "you are good; you don't despise me. You take me into your house; you light your candles for me, and I hav'n't hid from you where I come from, and how miserable I am."

The bishop, who was sitting near him, touched his hand gently and said: "You need not tell me who you are. This is not my house; it is the house of Christ. It does not ask any comer whether he has a name, but whether he has an affliction. You are suffering; you are hungry and thirsty; be welcome. And do not thank me; do not tell me that I take you into my house. This is the home of no man, except him who needs an asylum. I tell you, who are a traveller, that you are more at home here than I; whatever is here is yours. What need have I to know your name? Besides, before you told me, I knew it."

The man opened his eyes in astonishment:

"Really? You knew my name?"

"Yes," answered the bishop, "your name is my brother."

"Stop, stop, Monsieur Curé," exclaimed the man. "I was famished when I came in, but you are so kind that now I don't know what I am; that is all gone."

The bishop looked at him again and said:

"You have seen much suffering?"

"Oh, the red blouse, the ball and chain, the plank

to sleep on, the heat, the cold, the galley's crew, the lash, the double chain for nothing, the dungeon for a word, —even when sick in bed, the chain. The dogs, the dogs are happier! nineteen years! and I am forty-six, and now a yellow passport. That is all."

"Yes," answered the bishop, "you have left a place of suffering. But listen, there will be more joy in heaven over the tears of a repentant sinner, than over the white robes of a hundred good men. If you are leaving that sorrowful place with hate and anger against men, you are worthy of compassion; if you leave it with goodwill, gentleness, and peace, you are better than any of us."

Meantime Madame Magloire had served up supper; it consisted of soup made of water, oil, bread, and salt, a little port, a scrap of mutton, a few figs, a green cheese, and a large loaf of rye bread. She had, without asking, added to the usual dinner of the bishop a bottle of fine old Mauves wine.

The bishop's countenance was lighted up with this expression of pleasure, peculiar to hospitable natures. "To supper!" he said briskly, as was his habit when he had a guest. He seated the man at his right. Mademoiselle Baptistine, perfectly quiet and natural, took her place at his left.

The bishop said the blessing, and then served the soup himself, according to his usual custom. The man fell to, eating greedily.

Suddenly the bishop said: "It seems to me something is lacking on the table."

The fact was, that Madame Magloire had set out only

the three plates which were necessary. Now it was the custom of the house, when the bishop had any one to supper, to set all six of the silver plates on the table, an innocent display. This graceful appearance of luxury was a sort of childlikeness which was full of charm in this gentle but austere household, which elevated poverty to dignity.

Madame Magloire understood the remark; without a word she went out, and a moment afterwards the three plates for which the bishop had asked were shining on the cloth, symmetrically arranged before each of the three guests.

IV · *Tranquillity*

THE BISHOP WAS THE SAME AS ON OTHER EVE-
nings, from beginning to end. He took supper with
Jean Valjean with the same air and manner that he
would have supped with Monsieur Gédéon, the provost,
or with the curé of the parish.

Having finished the dessert, the bishop said grace, after
which he turned toward his guest and said: "You must
be in great need of sleep."

After having said good-night to his sister, Monseigneur Bienvenue took one of the silver candlesticks
from the table, handed the other to his guest, and said
to him:

"Monsieur, I will show you to your room."

The man followed him.

As may have been understood from what has been
said before, the house was so arranged that one could
reach the alcove in the oratory only by passing through
the bishop's sleeping chamber. Just as they were passing through this room Madame Magloire was putting
up the silver in the cupboard at the head of the bed.
It was the last thing she did every night before going
to bed.

The bishop left his guest in the alcove, before a clean

white bed. The man set down the candlestick upon a small table.

"Come," said the bishop, "a good night's rest to you; to-morrow morning, before you go, you shall have a cup of warm milk from our cows."

"Thank you, Monsieur," said the man.

When the alcove was occupied, a heavy serge curtain was drawn in the oratory, concealing the altar. Before this curtain the bishop knelt as he passed out, and offered a short prayer.

A moment afterwards he was walking in the garden, surrendering mind and soul to a dreamy contemplation of these grand and mysterious works of God, which night makes visible to the eye.

As to the man, he was so completely exhausted that he did not even avail himself of the clean white sheets; he blew out the candle with his nostril, after the manner of convicts, and fell on the bed, dressed as he was, into a sound sleep.

Midnight struck as the bishop came back to his chamber.

A few moments afterwards all in the little house slept.

V · *Jean Valjean*

TOWARDS THE MIDDLE OF THE NIGHT, JEAN VAL-
jean awoke.

He was of a thoughtful disposition, but not sad, which
is characteristic of affectionate natures. Upon the whole,
however, there was something torpid and insignificant,
in the appearance at least, of Jean Valjean. He had lost
his parents when very young. His mother died of mal-
practice in a milkfever: his father, a pruner before him,
was killed by a fall from a tree. Jean Valjean now had
but one relative left, his sister, a widow with seven
children, girls and boys. This sister had brought up
Jean Valjean, and, as long as her husband lived, she
had taken care of her younger brother. Her husband
died, leaving the eldest of these children eight, the
youngest one year old. Jean Valjean had just reached
his twenty-fifth year: he took the father's place, and,
in his turn, supported the sister who reared him.

He earned in the pruning season eighteen sous a day:
after that he hired out as a reaper, workman, teamster,
or labourer. He did whatever he could find to do. His
sister worked also, but what could she do with seven
little children? It was a sad group, which misery was
grasping and closing upon, little by little. There was a

very severe winter; Jean had no work, the family had no bread; literally, no bread, and seven children.

One Sunday night, Maubert Isabeau, the baker on the Place de l'Eglise, in Faverolles, was just going to bed when he heard a violent blow against the barred window of his shop. He got down in time to see an arm thrust through the aperture made by the blow of a fist on the glass. The arm seized a loaf of bread and took it out. Isabeau rushed out; the thief used his legs valiantly; Isabeau pursued him and caught him. The thief had thrown away the bread, but his arm was still bleeding. It was Jean Valjean.

All that happened in 1795. Jean Valjean was brought before the tribunals of the time for "burglary at night, in an inhabited house." He was found guilty. Jean Valjean was sentenced to five years in the galleys.

He was taken to Toulon, at which place he arrived after a journey of twenty-seven days, on a cart, a chain about his neck. At Toulon he was dressed in a red blouse, all his past life was effaced, even to his name. He was no longer Jean Valjean: he was Number 24,601. What became of his sister? Who troubled himself about that? What became of the seven children? What becomes of the handful of leaves of the young tree when it is sawn at the trunk?

Near the end of his fourth year, his chance of liberty came to Jean Valjean. His comrades helped him as they always do in that dreary place, and he escaped. He wandered two days in freedom through the fields; if it is freedom to be hunted, to turn your head each moment,

to tremble at the least noise, to be afraid of everything, of the smoke of a chimney, the passing of a man, the baying of a dog, the gallop of a horse, the striking of a clock, of the day because you see, and of the night because you do not; of the road, of the path, the bush, of sleep. During the evening of the second day he was retaken; he had neither eaten nor slept for thirty-six hours. The maritime tribunal extended his sentence three years for this attempt, which made eight. In the sixth year his turn of escape came again; he tried it, but failed again. He did not answer at roll-call, and the alarm cannon was fired. At night the people of the vicinity discovered him hidden beneath the keel of a vessel on the stocks; he resisted the galley guard which seized him. Escape and resistance. This the provisions of the special code punished by an addition of five years, two with the double chain, thirteen years. The tenth year his turn came round again; he made another attempt with no better success. Three years for this new attempt. Sixteen years. And finally, I think it was in the thirteenth year, he made yet another, and was retaken after an absence of only four hours. Three years for these four hours. Nineteen years. In October, 1815, he was set at large: he had entered in 1796 for having broken a pane of glass, and taken a loaf of bread.

Jean Valjean entered the galleys sobbing and shuddering: he went out hardened; he entered in despair: he went out sullen. From year to year this soul had withered more and more, slowly, but fatally. With this withered heart, he had a dry eye. When he left the galleys, he had not shed a tear for nineteen years.

When the time for leaving the galleys came, and when there were sounded in the ear of Jean Valjean the strange words: *You are free!* the moment seemed improbable and unreal; a ray of living light, a ray of the true light of living men, suddenly penetrated his soul. But this ray quickly faded away. Jean Valjean had been dazzled with the idea of liberty. He had believed in a new life. He soon saw what sort of liberty that is which has a yellow passport.

Liberation is not deliverance. A convict may leave the galleys behind, but not his condemnation.

VI · The Man Awakes

AS THE CATHEDRAL CLOCK STRUCK TWO, JEAN VAL-
jean awoke.

What awakened him was, too good a bed. For nearly
twenty years he had not slept in a bed, and, although
he had not undressed, the sensation was too novel not
to disturb his sleep.

He had slept something more than four hours. His
fatigue had passed away. He was not accustomed to give
many hours to repose.

He opened his eyes, and looked for a moment into
the obscurity about him, then he closed them to go to
sleep again.

When many diverse sensations have disturbed the
day, when the mind is preoccupied, we can fall asleep
once, but not a second time. Sleep comes at first much
more readily than it comes again. Such was the case
with Jean Valjean. He could not get to sleep again, and
so he began to think.

He was in one of those moods in which the ideas we
have in our minds are perturbed. There was a kind of
vague ebb and flow in his brain. His oldest and his
latest memories floated about pell mell, and crossed
each other confusedly, losing their own shapes, swelling
beyond measure, then disappearing all at once, as if in

a muddy and troubled stream. Many thoughts came to him, but there was one which continually presented itself, and which drove away all others. What that thought was, we shall tell directly. He had noticed the six silver plates and the large ladle that Madame Magliore had put on the table.

Those six silver plates took possession of him. There they were, within a few steps. At the very moment that he passed through the middle room to reach the one he was now in, the old servant was placing them in a little cupboard at the head of the bed. He had marked that cupboard well: on the right, coming from the dining-room. They were solid; and old silver. With the big ladle, they would bring at least two hundred francs, double what he had got for nineteen years' labour.

His mind wavered a whole hour, and a long one, in fluctuation and in struggle. The clock struck three. He opened his eyes, rose up hastily in bed, reached out his arm and felt his haversack, which he had put into the corner of the alcove, then he thrust out his legs and placed his feet on the ground, and found himself, he knew not how, seated on his bed.

He rose to his feet, hesitated for a moment longer, and listened; all was still in the house; he walked straight and cautiously towards the window, which he could discern. The night was not very dark; there was a full moon, across which large clouds were driving before the wind. This produced alternations of light and shade, out-of-doors eclipses and illuminations, and in-doors a kind of glimmer. This glimmer, enough to enable him

to find his way, changing with the passing clouds, re-sembled that sort of livid light, which falls through the window of a dungeon before which men are passing and repassing. On reaching the window, Jean Valjean examined it. It had no bars, opened into the garden, and was fastened, according to the fashion of the country, with a little sedge only. He opened it; but as the cold, keen air rushed into the room, he closed it again immediately. He looked into the garden with that absorbed look which studies rather than sees. The garden was enclosed with a white wall, quite low, and readily scaled. Beyond, against the sky, he distinguished the tops of trees at equal distances apart, which showed that this wall separated the garden from an avenue or a lane planted with trees.

When he had taken this observation, he turned like a man whose mind is made up, went to his alcove, took his haversack, opened it, fumbled in it, put his shoes into one of his pockets, tied up his bundle, swung it upon his shoulders, put on his cap, and pulled the vizor down over his eyes, felt for his stick, and went and put it in the corner of the window.

Holding his breath, with stealthy steps, he moved towards the door of the next room, which was the bishop's as we know. On reaching the door, he found it was unlatched. The bishop had not closed it.

VII · What He Does

JEAN VALJEAN LISTENED. NOT A SOUND.

He pushed the door.

He pushed it lightly with the end of his finger, with the stealthy and timorous carefulness of a cat. The door yielded to the pressure with a silent, imperceptible movement, which made the opening a little wider.

He waited a moment, and then pushed the door again more boldly.

It yielded gradually and silently. The opening was now wide enough for him to pass through; but there was a small table near the door which with it formed a troublesome angle, and which barred the entrance.

Jean Valjean saw the obstacle. At all hazards the opening must be made still wider.

He so determined, and pushed the door a third time, harder than before. This time a rusty hinge suddenly sent out into the darkness a harsh and prolonged creak.

Jean Valjean shivered. The noise of this hinge sounded in his ears as clear and terrible as the trumpet of the Judgment Day.

In the fantastic exaggeration of the first moment, he almost imagined that this hinge had become animate, and suddenly endowed with a terrible life; and that it was barking like a dog to warn everybody, and rouse the sleepers.

He stopped, shuddering and distracted, and dropped from his tiptoes to his feet. He felt the pulses of his temples beat like triphammers, and it appeared to him that his breath came from his chest with the roar of wind from a cavern.

He stood still, petrified like the pillar of salt, not daring to stir. Some minutes passed. The door was wide open; he ventured a look into the room. Nothing moved. He listened. Nothing was stirring in the house. The noise of the rusty hinge had wakened nobody.

This first danger was over, but still he felt within him a frightful tumult. Nevertheless he did not flinch. Not even when he thought he was lost had he flinched. His only thought was to make an end of it quickly. He took one step and was in the room.

Jean Valjean passed quickly, without looking at the bishop, along the bed, straight to the cupboard which he perceived near its head; he prepared to force the lock; the key was in it; he opened it; the first thing he saw was the basket of silver, he took it, crossed the room with hasty stride, careless of noise, reached the door, entered the oratory, took his stick, stepped out, put the silver in his knapsack, threw away the basket, ran across the garden, leaped over the wall like a tiger, and fled.

VIII · The Bishop at Work

THE NEXT DAY AT SUNRISE, MONSEIGNEUR BIEN-
venu was walking in the garden. Madame Magloire ran
towards him quite beside herself.

"Monseigneur, monseigneur," cried she, "Does your
greatness know where the silver basket is?"

"Yes," said the bishop.

"God be praised!" said she, "I did not know what had
become of it."

The bishop had just found the basket on a flower-bed.
He gave it to Madame Magloire and said: "There it is."

"Yes," she said, "but there is nothing in it. The silver?"

"Ah!" said the bishop, "it is the silver then that
troubles you. I do not know where that is."

"Good heavens! it is stolen. That man who came last
night stole it."

And in the twinkling of an eye, with all the agility
of which her age was capable, Madame Magloire ran to
the oratory, went into the alcove, and came back to the
bishop. The bishop was bending with some sadness over
a cochlearia des Guillons, which the basket had broken
in falling. He looked up at Madame Magloire's cry:

"Monseigneur, the man has gone! the silver is stolen!"

While she was uttering this exclamation her eyes fell
on an angle of the garden where she saw traces of an

escalade. A capstone of the wall had been thrown down.

"See, there is where he got out; he jumped into Cochefilet lane. The abominable fellow! he has stolen our silver!"

The bishop was silent for a moment, then raising his serious eyes, he said mildly to Madame Magloire:

"Now first, did this silver belong to us?"

Madame Magloire did not answer; after a moment the bishop continued:

"Madame Magloire, I have for a long time wrongfully withheld this silver; it belonged to the poor. Who was this man? A poor man evidently."

"Alas! alas!" returned Madame Magloire. "It is not on my account or mademoiselle's; it is all the same to us. But it is on yours, monseigneur. What is monsieur going to eat from now?"

The bishop looked at her with amazement:

"How so! have we no tin plates?"

Madame Magloire shrugged her shoulders.

"Tin smells."

"Well, then, iron plates."

Madame Magloire made an expressive gesture.

"Iron tastes."

"Well," said the bishop, "then, wooden plates."

In a few minutes he was breakfasting at the same table at which Jean Valjean sat the night before. While breakfasting, Monseigneur Bienvenu pleasantly remarked to his sister who said nothing, and Madame Magloire who was grumbling to herself, that there was really no need even for a wooden spoon or fork to dip a piece of bread into a cup of milk.

"Was there ever such an idea?" said Madame Magloire to herself, as she went backwards and forwards: "to take in a man like that, and to give him a bed beside him; and yet what a blessing it was that he did nothing but steal!"

Just as the brother and sister were rising from the table, there was a knock at the door.

"Come in," said the bishop.

The door opened. A strange, fierce group appeared on the threshold. Three men were holding a fourth by the collar. The three men were gendarmes; the fourth Jean Valjean.

A brigadier of gendarmes, who appeared to head the group, was near the door. He advanced towards the bishop, giving a military salute.

"Monseigneur," said he—

At this word Jean Valjean, who was sullen and seemed entirely cast down, raised his head with a stupefied air—

"Monseigneur!" he murmured, "then it is not the curé!"

"Silence!" said the gendarme, "it is monseigneur, the bishop."

In the meantime Monsieur Bienvenu had approached as quickly as his great age permitted:

"Ah, there you are!" said he, looking toward Jean Valjean, "I am glad to see you. But! I gave you the candlesticks also, which are silver like the rest, and would bring two hundred francs. Why did you not take them along with your plates?"

Jean Valjean opened his eyes and looked at the bishop with an expression which no human tongue could describe.

"Monseigneur," said the brigadier, "then what this man said was true? We met him. He was going like a man who was running away, and we arrested him in order to see. He had this silver."

"And he told you," interrupted the bishop, with a smile, "that it had been given him by a good old priest with whom he had passed the night. I see it all. And you brought him back here? It is all a mistake."

"If that is so," said the brigadier, "we can let him go."

"Certainly," replied the bishop.

The gendarmes released Jean Valjean, who shrank back—

"Is it true that they let me go?" he said in a voice almost inarticulate, as if he were speaking in his sleep.

"Yes! you can go. Do you not understand?" said a gendarme.

"My friend," said the bishop, "before you go away, here are your candlesticks; take them."

He went to the mantelpiece, took the two candlesticks, and brought them to Jean Valjean. The two women beheld the action without a word, or gesture, or look, that might disturb the bishop.

Jean Valjean was trembling in every limb. He took the two candlesticks mechanically, and with a wild appearance.

"Now," said the bishop, "go in peace. By the way, my friend, when you come again, you need not come through the garden. You can always come in and go out by the front door. It is closed only with a latch, day or night."

Then turning to the gendarmes, he said:

"Messieurs, you can retire." The gendarmes withdrew.

Jean Valjean felt like a man who is just about to faint.

The bishop approached him, and said, in a low voice:

"Forget not, never forget that you have promised me to use this silver to become an honest man."

Jean Valjean, who had no recollection of this promise, stood confounded. The bishop had laid much stress upon these words as he uttered them. He continued, solemnly:

"Jean Valjean, my brother: you belong no longer to evil, but to good. It is your soul that I am buying for you. I withdraw it from dark thoughts and from the spirit of perdition, and I give it to God!"

IX · *The Man Weeps*

WHEN JEAN VALJEAN LEFT THE BISHOP'S HOUSE,
his mood was one that he had never known before. He
could understand nothing of what was passing within
him. He set himself stubbornly in opposition to the
angelic deeds and the gentle words of the old man, "you
have promised me to become an honest man. I am
purchasing your soul, I withdraw it from the spirit of
perversity, and I give it to God Almighty." This came
back to him incessantly. To this celestial tenderness, he
opposed pride, which is the fortress of evil in man. He
felt dimly that the pardon of this priest was the hardest
assault, and the most formidable attack which he had
yet sustained; that his hardness of heart would be com-
plete, if it resisted this kindness; that if he yielded, he
must renounce that hatred with which the acts of other
men had for so many years filled his soul, and in which
he found satisfaction; that, this time, he must conquer or
be conquered, and that the struggle, a gigantic and decisive struggle, had begun between his own wickedness,
and the goodness of this man.

In view of all these things, he moved like a drunken
man. While thus walking on with haggard look, had he
a distinct perception of what might be to him the result
of his adventure at D———? Did he hear those

mysterious murmurs which warn or entreat the spirit at certain moments of life? Did a voice whisper in his ear that he had just passed through the decisive hour of his destiny, that there was no longer a middle course for him, that if, thereafter, he should not be the best of men, he would be the worst, that he must now, so to speak, mount higher than the bishop, or fall lower than the galley slave; that, if he would become good, he must become an angel; that, if he would remain wicked, he must become a monster?

He fell exhausted upon a great stone, his hands clenched in his hair, and his face on his knees. Then his heart swelled, and he burst into tears. It was the first time he had wept for nineteen years.

Jean Valjean wept long. He shed hot tears, he wept bitterly, with more weakness than a woman, with more terror than a child.

While he wept, the light grew brighter and brighter in his mind—an extraordinary light, a light at once transporting and terrible. His past life, his first offence, his long expiation, his brutal exterior, his hardened interior, his release made glad by so many schemes of vengeance, what had happened to him at the bishop's, all this returned and appeared to him, clearly, but in a light that he had never seen before. He beheld his life, and it seemed to him horrible; his soul, and it seemed to him frightful. There was however, a softened light upon that life and upon that soul. It seemed to him that he was looking upon Satan by the light of Paradise.

How long did he weep thus? What did he do after

weeping? Where did he go? Nobody ever knew. It is known simply that, on that night, the stage-driver who drove the Grenoble route, saw, as he passed through the bishop's street, a man in the attitude of prayer, kneel upon the pavement in the shadow, before the door of Monseigneur Bienvenu.